Book of the Film

This edition published by Parragon in 2013
Parragon
Chartist House
15–17 Trim Street
Bath BA1 1HA, UK
www.parragon.com

Adapted by Sarah Nathan
Teleplay by Vince Marcello & Mark Landry and Robert Horn
Story by Vince Marcello & Mark Landry

ISBN 978-1-4723-1886-2

Printed in UK

Book of the Film

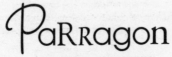

Bath · New York · Singapore · Hong Kong · Cologne · Delhi
Melbourne · Amsterdam · Johannesburg · Shenzhen

Chapter 1

The sun shone brightly on a California beach on a perfect surfing day. The conditions were just right for catching waves. Many surfers were carving up breakers on their boards. Brady, a blond surfer, was right in the middle of the action. His girlfriend McKenzie – Mack to her friends – came up behind him. Brady smiled at her as they both expertly rode a wave in.

Mack broke away from Brady and cut sharply down the face of the wave. She crouched down and grabbed the edge of the board with her hand as the wave folded over her. Inside the wave, she felt the thrill of taking command of her board.

As she shot out of the water barrel, she sped past Brady. Mack loved surfing – *and* teasing her boyfriend. She glanced over her shoulder at him and waved. He took the challenge and followed her lead.

After a few hours of surfing, a stunning sunset spread out across the sky. Brady and Mack walked along the water's edge together carrying their surfboards.

Brady looked over at Mack and grinned. "Best day ever!" he exclaimed.

"It was pretty awesome, huh?" Mack replied.

"*Awesome?*" he replied. "Surfing all day? Us being together? Awesome *wishes* it was this awesome!" He stopped and looked into Mack's eyes. "This has been the perfect summer."

Mack looked around, taking in the beautiful beach sunset. "It *has* been perfect," she said. Then she looked down. The tide was going out and her feet were slowly sinking into the wet sand. "It's just, the thing is, Brady...."

She stopped herself. She had something to tell him, but she couldn't get the words out. When she glanced back at Brady, he was looking at the horizon.

"Hey, check it out!" he shouted.

Following his gaze, Mack spotted the huge wave travelling towards the shore. "Those swells must be breaking at, what, forty feet?" she asked, squinting.

"I read there's a gnarly storm coming in from up north," Brady replied, keeping his eyes on the ocean. "Same time as the trade winds are hitting."

"Surf like this happens once every ten years!" Mack exclaimed. "Imagine dropping into a barrel that intense!"

Brady flashed her a smile. "Luckily, we've still got a whole week left of vacation to enjoy it."

Mack took a deep breath. What she had wanted to tell him would ruin this sunset – and this moment. And the promise of a great surfing day tomorrow made the night even sweeter. She decided to change the subject. "Come on. I'm starving," she said.

Together, they took off for the beach surf shop up ahead. The shop belonged to Mack's grandfather and was where he crafted custom-built surfboards.

"First thing tomorrow, we hit the beach and that awesome surf," Brady said. "Imagine what you'll do on waves that heavy – carving, kick flips, laybacks!"

"Brady, about tomorrow...." Mack began as she walked into the surf shop.

"No way!" Brady cried, pushing past her. On the television was an old 1960s surf movie. The surfer on screen was doing amazing trick handstands on his surfboard!

"I can't believe you're watching this without me!" Brady complained to Mack's grandfather.

"Now that you're here, I'm not," the older man replied. He winked at his granddaughter.

Mack watched as a girl came out of the water with her hair still perfect – and completely dry. Rolling her eyes, Mack sighed. Even the water was fake in these old beach movies! "Please tell me it isn't...."

"*Wet Side Story!*" Brady and Mack's grandfather answered in unison.

"1962. Surfers. Bikers. Best movie ever made," Brady declared. His eyes were glued to the screen.

"How can you two like that silliness?" she asked, looking from Brady to her grandfather. "Especially you, Grandpa." Mack gave him a stern look.

"Silliness?" her grandfather asked. He shook his head. "Mack, my dear, this movie defined an entire culture."

"Exactly," Brady jumped in. "A surfer guy and a biker girl share a secret love while trying to unite their rival gangs, as an evil real estate mogul tries to turn their hangout into a resort by building a weather machine that blows up, creating a massive storm." He raised his eyebrows high. "Silliness? *Really?*"

"The boy makes a good point," Mack's grandfather said.

"Fine, but can you watch it later? I really need to talk to you...." Mack said, pulling on Brady's elbow.

Brady's eyes were still fixed on the television. On screen, a group of surfers ran into Big Momma's Bungalow. It was a beach hangout decorated with surfboards and shells. There were surfers sitting on one side of the restaurant and bikers on the other side.

"Just check out my favourite part," Brady urged. "When the two leads – Lela's and Tanner's – eyes meet, they're pulled apart by their two conflicting rival gangs." Brady pointed to the TV. "Look!"

Mack watched Lela, a biker chick, and Tanner, a surfer, sing a song about falling in love.

Lela was singing on stage until she teetered too close to the edge and fell! She tumbled right into Tanner's arms.

"Hey, get your soggy surfer mitts off my baby sister!" one of the biker dudes shouted towards the group of surfers.

As the surfers and bikers circled each other, Lela and Tanner locked eyes. Mack crossed her arms over her chest and rolled her eyes again.

"I love this part," Mack's grandfather confessed.

"It's classic," Brady agreed.

"Come *on*," Mack said, exasperated. "They sing for no reason! When they come out of the water, their hair is totally dry! The girls never surf as well as the boys. *And* they sing for no reason. I mention that again because even the second time, I don't get why."

Brady glanced over at Mack. "But it *is* always summer, and everybody just dances and surfs."

Mack shrugged. "Well, sure, the surfing part sounds fun...."

Just then, there was a knock at the front door. When Mack went to see who was there, her grandfather had a worried look on his face. He grabbed the remote and turned off the TV.

"But, come on. They sing *in* the ocean and never spit out water!" Mack called over her shoulder. She opened the door and then froze. Standing in the doorway was Mack's Aunt Antoinette – a businesswoman who definitely didn't look like she fit into the laid-back surfing scene.

"How about giving your Aunt Antoinette a hug?" she asked, smiling. Mack grinned and threw her arms round her aunt.

"You're so grown up," Antoinette cooed. She stood back and looked at her niece in her bikini. "You look absolutely ... unacceptable."

"Excuse me?" Mack said, offended.

"Not you, dear!" Antoinette said quickly. She pointed to her earpiece and continued on with her business call. "Tell him the offer is unacceptable." She clicked off the phone and turned to Mack. "It's good to see you!" she sang sweetly.

"What are you doing here?" Mack asked. "I thought you were coming tomorrow."

Antoinette shook her head. "Then you thought wrong. We're *leaving* tomorrow."

Brady walked towards the door. "Mack, what does she mean by leaving tomorrow?"

"Brady, I'm McKenzie's aunt," Antoinette said, extending her hand. "I'm sure she's told you all about me."

Brady turned to Mack. "What does she mean by leaving tomorrow?" he repeated.

"Welcome home, Antoinette," Mack's grandfather said, walking towards her.

"Hello, Father," Antoinette replied.

"Glad to have you home," he said kindly.

Antoinette looked past her father into the shop. "Doesn't look like much has changed around here. I see you're still making surfboards."

"The best surfboards on the beach!" Mack said, proudly.

"You know, I could get you a great price on this place," Antoinette said, gesturing to the prime beach location. "Of course, we'd have to tear it down first." She scanned the old shop and her eyes settled on a vintage surfboard hanging over the entrance. "Don't tell me you still have *that*?"

"Still *have* it?" Mack asked incredulously. She looked up lovingly at the old surfboard with the carved rose emblem. "We all grew up on the mythical legends of this board. This board is part of the family."

"Me, your grandfather, his father ... we each found our destiny on it," her grandfather said.

"There's only one way to find your destiny in this world," Antoinette snorted. "And that's to work for it."

Brady jumped in. "Okay, not meaning to sound redundant, but – what does she mean by leaving tomorrow?"

Antoinette leaned in closer to Brady. Her face was beaming with pride. "Brady, starting tomorrow, my niece will be attending the prestigious, overpriced Dunwich Prep School back east." She pointed at Mack. "Anyone who's *anyone* in the corporate world went there."

Brady's mouth fell open. "What?"

"Antoinette, we should talk about this," Mack's grandfather said quietly.

"This was always the deal," she snapped. She looked at her niece. "Isn't that right McKenzie?"

Mack felt trapped. She couldn't breathe. "Sure," she said. "It's just ... tomorrow there are these extreme conditions I've been waiting my entire life to surf –"

Cutting her off, Antoinette put her arm round her. "Surf? Sweetheart, your new life begins as of our morning flight. That's what's important, not some surf."

Mack couldn't even respond. She ducked out of her aunt's embrace and ran up to her room.

A few moments later, Brady appeared at her bedroom door. "I can't believe you didn't tell me," he said quietly.

"You don't know how hard I tried," Mack said, looking down at her feet. "I just didn't know how."

Brady sat down on Mack's bed. "So, you're leaving for a private school? Just like that? Why are they making you do this?"

Mack shook her head. "They're not making me. It's my choice."

"So, change your mind!" Brady exclaimed. "I do it all the time. No, I don't. Yes, I do. See?"

"It's too late," Mack confessed. "My flight is at noon tomorrow."

"How can you leave?" Brady pressed her. "This is your home. It's where your grandfather is, where you surf, where I am!"

Mack took a deep breath. "I was really lucky to get into this school. My aunt says it will pave the way for my future.

"I know you're upset," she continued. "I should have told you."

"And what is this 'deal' your aunt was talking about?" he asked.

"After we lost my mum, the deal was I would stay here with my grandfather through the first part of high school," she explained. "Then, when it was time to get more serious, I'd go to this school, like my aunt did."

The explanation didn't make Brady feel any better. "So she just shows up to take you away?" he asked. "Aren't you happy here?"

Getting up, Mack crossed the room and lifted the lid of an old trunk. Inside was her memory box. She gently opened the box and took out a worn, tattered book, wrapped in fabric. She held it carefully. "This was my mum's journal," she explained.

Brady went over to her. "What does it say?" he asked.

Opening to a marked page, Mack read from

the journal entry. "'Most of all, I dream my daughter becomes a great success. That she isn't just pulled through life, but marches through it triumphantly.'"

"She sounds like she was amazing," Brady said.

Mack closed the book. "My mum wanted to go to college and make something of herself, but then she had me, and time passed, and then...." Mack looked out the window as she collected her thoughts. "She never got to live out that dream."

"But that's not your fault," Brady told her.

"I know it's not, but I also know that I can do what she never got a chance to," she said softly.

Brady reached for Mack. "That doesn't mean you have to be what your aunt is. You can be anything you want!"

Mack looked down at the journal in her hands. "This is what I have to do," she said. "It's what she wanted. Please try to understand."

"And what about us?" Brady asked.

Mack paused. "How can there be an 'us' after today?" she said in a low voice.

"I'll wait for you," he said.

Mack found the strength to look up. "Brady, I know what it feels like to miss someone. I care about you too much to ever put you through that."

"So you're saying you care about me enough to break up with me?" he asked. He stood up and backed away.

"I don't want to, but what choice do I have?" She gave him a kiss on the cheek. "Thanks for the most awesome summer of my life. I wish it wasn't over. I wish *we* weren't over."

Brady walked sadly out of the room. As Mack watched him go, she noticed a photo of herself and Brady taken earlier in the summer. She picked up the photograph and slid it into her suitcase. She closed her eyes and sighed. Leaving was going to be much harder than she had thought.

Chapter 2

As the sun rose the next morning, Mack sat on her bed staring at her suitcases. She wasn't ready to say goodbye.

Outside her door, her grandfather leaned the surfboard with the rose emblem against the wall. When he walked away, the rose in the centre started to glow mysteriously.

As soon as she opened her door, Mack saw the surfboard and smiled. She quickly scribbled a note to her grandfather. Mack knew that he would understand her need for a last-minute surf run. She couldn't leave without one more ride.

The conditions were perfect. Mack checked

out the waves and couldn't wait to get in the water. As she squinted in the sunlight, she spotted Brady walking towards her.

"How did you know I was here?" she asked.

"I knew you couldn't stay away from surf like this," he said.

"I'm glad you came, but...." Mack said, her voice trailing off. She shifted her feet. "I told you, we aren't –"

Brady grinned at her. "It's okay," he told her. "I'm just here to watch you surf, not to propose."

Lifting up her board, Mack ran to the shoreline. "Then check out what I'm about to do!" She paddled out beyond the reef and waited patiently for a wave to come rolling in. It was aggressive surf, but Mack held her stance and rode the wave in. The waves kept coming and Mack was ready every time. She expertly ripped across each wave.

Mack's grandfather walked out of his surf shop and stood on the cool sand. He searched the beach for Mack and saw her riding the waves with a few other surfers. He couldn't help but notice the dark clouds on the horizon.

"You've got to see this," Brady called to Mack's grandfather. "She's ripping it!"

"I don't like the look of that sky, Brady," her grandfather said worriedly.

"You're right," Brady replied. "It looks bad. They'd better get out of there."

At that moment, the lifeguard stood up and blew his whistle. He raised a red flag and signalled that everyone had to get out of the water. All the surfers headed back in – except Mack.

Brady shielded his eyes and pointed to Mack. "What is she doing?"

"She's not paddling in," her grandfather said, concerned.

A huge wave was building and heading right for Mack!

But Mack knew exactly what she was doing. She was waiting for the ride of her life!

The huge wave continued to gain strength and power. It was unlike anything Mack had ever seen. A perfect barrel was cresting at an amazing height, calling any surfer who had the guts to attempt the ride. Mack was ready.

When Brady realized what Mack was doing, he sprang into action. He ran to a Jet Ski lying on the sand, grabbed a lifejacket and rode out towards Mack. "Don't do it, Mack!" he cried as he reached her.

"I have to!" she called back. She turned to face the growing wave. This was her moment and she was totally focused.

A hush fell across the beach. All eyes were on Mack.

"Insane!" a surfer on the beach shouted. "She's going to try to carve that monster!"

Mack paddled straight into the rising wave. She was more determined than ever. At the right moment, she stood up and positioned her feet in a surfing stance. She was high on the wave, but then she suddenly dropped down the vertical wall of water in a free fall. Somehow, she regained control in a spectacular move, but Brady knew more was coming. He gunned his Jet Ski.

Everyone on the beach was cheering. Mack's skills were impressive and the whole crowd was watching in awe – except for her grandfather and Brady.

As the monster wave crashed over Mack's head, the force of the water pulled her deep beneath the surface. No matter which direction she turned, she saw only foam and swirling water. There was no way out. With an intense and powerful push, Mack was pulled away from her board.

Brady dived off his Jet Ski into the churning waves to help her. He fought the strong current as he tried to find Mack.

Onshore, the crowd was silent. Mack's grandfather looked out at the angry ocean. He waited for Mack and Brady to break the surface, but there was no sign of them.

Chapter 3

A few moments later, Mack's surfboard surfaced above the waves. Then Mack and Brady both came up, gasping for air.

They made their way to the shore and staggered onto the beach. Mack pulled her surfboard along behind her. Now that she was safe, she turned angrily to Brady.

"What did you do?" Mack shrieked.

"I tried to save you!" Brady exclaimed.

Mack stamped her foot in the sand. "I didn't need saving! This was my last chance to ride that monster wave before I left forever. And instead, I end up back here at ... at...."

Mack stopped talking and looked around. Everything looked ... different.

Who were those boys singing? And why was everyone wearing vintage 1960s beachwear?

"Okay," she said slowly, feeling very confused. "I must have hit my head. Is this what a concussion looks like?"

Brady looked around the beach. He took in the singing and dancing surfers in old-fashioned bathing suits. Brady turned back to focus on Mack. "Did we *both* hit our heads?" he asked.

A chorus of dancers was heading their way. Brady grabbed Mack's hand and together they dived behind a sailboat lodged on the sand. They got out of the way of the dancers just in time.

"It's weird," Brady said, peering over the side of the boat. He scratched his head. "I've been here before."

More and more surfers poured onto the beach and joined in the performance. Mack grabbed Brady's arm in a panic. "Maybe we're dead. We've died and ended up in a musical!"

A group of surfers suddenly lined up in front of them.

"Ka-razy!" a surfer named Seacat cried as he raced by Mack and Brady.

"Ka-razy!" the chorus of surfers answered.

This *is* ka-razy! Mack thought as the flash mob started to dance.

Just then, a group of girls in bikinis ran by, laughing. All the surfers watched them pass.

"Check that out," Seacat said with a whistle. "Only thing better than a wave crashing is a *wahine* walking!"

"In your dreams, Seacat," a surfer girl replied. "You've been hit on the head by too many boards!"

One of Seacat's friends jokingly pushed him, and they all laughed as they headed to the ocean.

Brady tugged on Mack's arm. His eyes were wide. "Mack!" Brady exclaimed. "We're *in* the movie!"

"In what movie?" Mack asked.

"*My* movie. *Wet Side Story*!" he exclaimed.

"What? How? Why?" she sputtered. At that moment, Mack realized why the blonde surfer who was leading the song looked so familiar. He was the star of the movie she had seen on TV! "What should we do?" she cried.

A smile spread across Brady's face. "For right now, I guess ... have some fun?"

"Any other options?" Mack asked.

"Look," Brady told her. "Somehow we are in my favourite movie ever, and a gang of singing surfers is heading this way." He stopped talking and pointed. "I say let's join in!" he shouted and he jumped into the dance.

The cast of surfers all announced their names as they lined up for a roll call. At the end of the line, Brady and Mack meekly mumbled their names as well.

"Check it out!" Brady shouted to Mack as he danced. He clapped and spun round at exactly the same time as the others. "I know all the moves!"

Mack stood back and watched Brady master the beach choreography. At the end of the dance, everyone fell to the sand. Mack sighed, happy that all that singing and dancing was over. But one more beat made the surfers sit up, put their sunglasses on and then fall back down. Mack tried to remain calm.

"This is fantastic," Brady gushed. "Crazy, right?"

"I'd say so," Mack replied.

Brady took her hand. "Come on!" He dragged Mack up to the crowd of surfers as they gathered at Big Momma's, the beach-hut restaurant from the film.

"No shirts, no shoes – no service!" Big Momma shouted from the front door. She smiled at all the surfers.

Suddenly, the group noticed Mack and Brady. The couple looked out of place in their futuristic beachwear. Brady felt all eyes on him.

"We haven't seen you kahunas around here before," Giggles, a surfer girl, said.

"I'm McKenzie," Mack said, trying to smile. "People call me Mack."

"I'm Brady. People call me ... Brady."

Seacat stood next to Brady. "And where are you cats from?"

Brady flashed a smile. "We're from ... uh ..." he began, "not far away." At the same time, Mack said, "Far away."

Oops. They gave each other a look. "Far away," Brady corrected himself, while Mack said, "Not far away" instead. Again, *oops.*

"Sorry," Brady said quickly. "We're still dealing with a major time change."

"Hey Rascal," Seacat said to his buddy next to him. "It seems like we've got some unwanted ho-dads we need to put the kibosh on!"

Brady reacted fast. "No, you got it all wrong!" he exclaimed.

Seacat shook his head. "We don't jelly roll to

outsiders," he told him.

As the group closed in on Brady and Mack, there was a loud rumble outside the restaurant. Brady suddenly realized what was happening. He reached for Mack and took her hand.

"This is Big Momma's," Brady told her. "The restaurant where the surfers and bikers hang."

At that moment, the door swung open and a biker loomed in the doorway. The biker pulled out a comb from his pocket and ran it smoothly through his hair.

Recalling the plot of the movie, Brady leaned in to Mack. "Each gang wants the other gone so they can have this place for themselves."

Another biker entered the restaurant. She had big hair and high-heeled shoes. She popped a large bubblegum bubble as she struck a pose.

Brady anxiously watched the door, waiting for the next biker to enter. "Here comes Butchy, the leader of the greaser motorcycle gang, the Rodents," he told Mack.

Mack stared at the bikers. "The Rodents?" she asked. Then a souped-up motorcycle rolled through the doorway and Butchy stepped inside.

"How cool is that!" Brady gasped. His mouth hung open.

"So ... we landed in the middle of a surf-and-turf war?" Mack asked.

Butchy snapped his fingers and clapped three times. Heeding the call, the bikers fell into formation round him. They all wore leather jackets with 'Rodents' painted on the back.

"Surfers!" Butchy complained, wrinkling up his nose. "I *knew* I smelled something fishy."

Seacat stepped forwards. "Rodents," he snarled. "I knew I should have laid some traps!"

Giggles put her hands on her hips. "I thought you were exterminated," she commented.

"And I thought you *surfers* were all washed up," one of the bikers shot back.

"Yeah," Butchy said, smiling. "'Cause clearly you is *drips!*"

"Why don't you make like the ocean and *wave* goodbye!" the surfer next to Seacat said.

Mack rolled her eyes. Between the bad grammar and the terrible lines, she was losing it!

Brady poked Mack and grinned. "They just don't write 'em like that anymore!"

"I do believes you alls is on *our* side of Big Momma's," Butchy said to Seacat and the surfers.

Seacat moved closer. "Yeah? And which side is your side?"

Butchy steadied his gaze at Seacat. "The left side!" he growled.

Tanner walked over to Butchy and put his hands on his shoulders. He turned the biker round to face the other side of the restaurant. "There!" he shouted.

All the surfers laughed – and so did Brady. Then he caught Mack's eye. "Oh, come on," he said. "That's great stuff!" He continued to say the lines with the characters as they argued.

By the jukebox, a biker took off her helmet. Mack looked closer and recognized her as Lela, the lead biker girl from the movie. Lela dropped a coin in the jukebox and then expertly kicked it so music began. Brady took Mack's hand and pulled her away. "Stand back!" he cried. When Mack protested, Brady replied, "You'll see!"

The music started and the bikers went into their dance routine, with Butchy singing the lead. Brady saw a Rodent leather jacket on the back of a chair and quickly pulled it on. Then, he hopped onto the table and started singing. Butchy, watching Brady approvingly, handed him an electric guitar. Brady slung the guitar over his shoulder, jumped off the table and then slid across the room on his knees.

Mack watched in disbelief. Since when did Brady know how to do all of these dance moves?

At the end of the song, Brady wound up face to face with Butchy. Butchy held out his hand to shake, but Brady went to give him a high five.

As a '60s biker, Butchy had no idea what to do. He thought Brady was going to smack him! Butchy put up his fists to fight back.

Taking this as a good exit cue, Mack pulled Brady out of the restaurant.

"You just couldn't help yourself, could you?" Mack said once they were outside.

"I've always wanted to be in that number," Brady replied sheepishly.

Mack sat down on the sand and rubbed her head. How were they ever going to get home?

Chapter 4

Mack gazed out at the ocean and listened to the familiar rhythm of the waves crashing on the beach. She sighed and turned to face Brady. "Remember that movie about the robot that drank liquid from an abandoned spaceship?" she asked. "And turned into a vampire middle-school teacher who taught the entire school how to salsa, and they went on to win the regional championship?"

"Yeah?" Brady replied, vaguely remembering the movie.

"That makes more sense than all this," she said, shaking her head.

Brady put up his hand. "I have an idea. Hand me my phone."

Mack raised her eyebrows and waited for Brady to realize what he had asked.

"What year was this movie made?" she asked.

"Around 1960," he said. "And?"

"And you're going to do what with a *mobile* phone?"

"Call my folks," Brady replied, and then he stopped. "Who weren't born yet. Right." He slumped back on the sand.

Mack tried to get Brady to focus. "Brady, my entire future is dependent on getting out of here, like, now!"

A bunch of surfers ran by them laughing as they headed towards the water.

Brady watched them hop on surfboards and paddle out to the waves. "*Except*, maybe it would be fun to hang here for a bit," he said.

"Except no, it wouldn't," Mack told him, "because I snuck out of my house and have to catch a plane in two hours. Well, two hours and fifty *years*."

Realizing how serious Mack was about leaving, Brady sighed. "Maybe we just need to figure out how we got here, so we can leave," he said. "Right before we landed here, we got caught in that storm. Maybe that had something to do with it?"

"So we need another storm to happen in order to leave," Mack said, thinking out loud.

Brady brightened. "We're in luck, because at the end of the movie, there's a *huge* storm."

Mack narrowed her eyes. "And what are we supposed to do in the meantime?"

A smile crept across his face. "Wait for the end of the movie!"

Putting her head in her hands, Mack moaned. "I knew it was a mistake to sneak out," she grumbled. "I should never have done it."

"You had to surf and you know it," Brady assured her. "You have to do what your heart tells you, Mack."

Just then, Seacat and a few surfers came running over to them.

"We're having a shredder shindig tonight here at Big Momma's," Seacat told them. "You should both make the scene."

"Thanks, but –" Mack began to say.

Brady put his hand on Mack's arm. "Actually, it sounds blastin'!" he exclaimed.

The surfers ran off as Mack gave Brady a stern look. "We're stuck in another dimension, and you think going to a party is the best use of our time?" She stood up. "Well, not me!"

At that moment, the daylight faded and suddenly it was evening. Instead of their bathing suits, Mack and Brady were wearing vintage 1960s beachwear.

"Where did these outfits come from?" Mack asked, slightly freaked out.

"The magic of movies," Brady said, winking.

Mack gave up trying to figure this all out. She headed inside Big Momma's with Brady.

On stage, a band was playing. There were a few surfers already dancing.

"This scene is great," Brady said to Mack. Then he realized where they were standing. He spotted the front door and pulled Mack away. "Heads up!" he cried.

Just then, two surfers ran through the entrance with their boards.

"No surfboards!" Big Momma called out.

A few bikers were standing towards the back of the restaurant. When they saw the surfers, they grimaced.

"Hey Lugnut, are you thinking what I'm thinking?" Butchy, the leader of the bikers, said to the boy next to him.

"That if you sneeze and cough at the same time, you could blow your whole face off?" Lugnut asked.

"No," Butchy said. He paused and thought about what Lugnut had said. "Well, yeah, but no! I'm thinking how much I don't like surfers."

"So boss, how we going to get Big Momma's to be only a biker joint?" Lugnut asked.

"Shut up, I'm thinking," Butchy snapped.

Cheechee, another one of the bikers, grunted. "How long is that going to take?"

"Great. Now I got two things to think about," Butchy grumbled. Then he shook his head. "Come on," Butchy said. "We is not gonna let a bunch of waterlogged washouts spoil our very fine *ev-e-ning*."

As soon as the bikers entered Big Momma's, the surfing dance party stopped.

Lela walked over with a tray of drinks and sat next to Butchy.

"Sodas for everyone," Lela said, smiling.

"Thanks, sis," Butchy said. "These surfers weren't bothering you, were they?"

"Of course not," Lela said to her big brother. "They're not so bad."

"*All* surfers is bad," Cheechee snapped.

"Except the ones that are *very* bad," Butchy

added. "They're even worse!" A few moments later, Big Momma walked in from the kitchen. Rascal spotted her and called her over.

"Hey Big Momma, you sure know how to fry up a fish burger," he said.

Big Momma smiled. "If you can catch it, Big Momma can cook it! It's home cooking because being here is like being home. Everyone is welcome here!"

Rascal reached out for Big Momma's hand and started dancing with her. Lela jumped onstage with a few backup singers and launched into a song.

Brady tried to join in and Mack had to practically drag him off the dance floor.

"I'm sorry, Brady, but I'm worried," she whispered. "I don't have time to wait for a storm. I'm going to the beach to see if I can figure another way out of here."

Brady spun her round. "But look!" he cried. "Remember? This is the part of the movie we saw at your grandfather's, where the two leads get together."

Mack headed for the door. "You enjoy it. I'll let you know if I come up with anything."

As Mack turned to leave, she bumped right into Tanner. His eyes met hers and they locked gazes.

At the same time, across the room, Lela stumbled and fell off the edge of the stage. Brady rushed over, and Lela fell into his arms. Their eyes met and she smiled. Lela sang the rest of the song directly to Brady.

When the music stopped, Lela stayed near Brady. "You totally saved my life," she said.

"Not really," Brady told her. "The stage is like, two feet up. The worst you would have done is broken a nail."

Lela flashed him a smile. "I guess I *literally* fell for you, huh?" she cooed. "I'm Lela."

At that moment, Brady realized that his on-screen crush was now standing in front of him! "I *know*," he admitted. "I mean, it's *really* you. I mean, I've thought about meeting you since I was, like, in fifth grade!"

"Me too!" Lela gushed. Then she paused. "Who are you?"

"I'm Brady, knight in shining board shorts." He puffed out his chest.

"That's a really long last name," she said, slightly puzzled.

Meanwhile, Tanner was still staring at Mack.

"Nice of you to drop in," he joked.

"Sorry, I didn't see you," she said, distracted. She tried to move towards the door.

"And now that you do, you like what you see?" Tanner asked with a wink.

"Oh, sure, nice to meet you," Mack said. She couldn't help but notice how cute he was. That is until she looked past him to the door and spotted Brady and Lela. Brady was practically drooling over her!

"Will you excuse me?" She walked up to Brady.

"Brady, can I have a moment?" When Brady didn't seem to hear her, Mack tried again. "A really quick, important moment?"

Reluctantly, Brady stepped away. "Excuse me, Lela," he said, apologetically.

"It was really great falling into you. We should do it again sometime," Lela flirted.

Mack leaned into Brady. She tried to act casual. "The mannequin with the six rows of teeth ... just asked me out."

But Brady wasn't listening. "Mack, something's not right," he said slowly.

Mack rolled her eyes. "We could make a list of the things that aren't right, starting with the fact that there are enough things for a list."

Brady shook his head. "Look around," he told her. He spun her round to see what was going on in the restaurant.

The room had suddenly grown eerily quiet. The surfers and bikers were each doing their own thing on opposite sides of the room.

"Nothing's happening," Brady explained. "It's almost ... dull."

Mack was confused. "Okay, and?" she asked.

Brady grabbed her shoulders. "In the movie, Lela sings that song about falling for the perfect boy and being happy."

Mack interrupted him. "See? That's my point. Why does she need a boy to be happy?"

"Because it's 1962," Brady answered. "The thing is, after Lela sings her song and falls off the stage, it is Tanner who is supposed to catch her as he's walking by."

"And what happens right after he catches her?" Mack asked.

"They fall instantly in love," Brady said. "But they're pulled apart and a full-on dance war breaks out."

Mack and Brady looked around Big Momma's. No one was dancing. There was no declared war. Everyone actually looked a little bit bored.

"It's almost like no one knows exactly what to do next," Mack guessed. She dragged Brady outside to the porch to talk more. "So Lela and Tanner were supposed to fall into each other's arms, find love, then be pulled apart in a turf war? That's how it's written?"

"But instead they fell into *our* arms and now they're into *us*," Brady concluded.

"And there's no turf war?" Mack asked. "So, we changed the movie?"

"We changed the movie," Brady confirmed.

"We changed the movie," Mack repeated.

Brady laughed and shook his head. "Yeah, third time, still doesn't sound too good, huh?"

Mack looked out onto the beach. "Do you think it will affect anything?"

Brady considered the question carefully. "It affected who they fell for. Who knows what else it could affect?"

Mack paced up and down the restaurant's porch to gather her thoughts. "Brady, you said there's a storm at the end of the movie that we can ride out of here on."

Brady followed her. "Yeah. Three days after they meet," he said.

Mack stopped walking. "Okay. I'm going to ask you something, even though I know, and I know you know, I don't want to know. Is there anything that happens in the next three days that somehow affects that storm?"

The colour started to slowly drain from Brady's face. "Come on," he said, racing down the porch steps to the sand. "Come on!"

Mack didn't take that as a good sign. "See? Didn't want to know!" she cried as she followed him down the beach. She hoped that Brady was on to something that could send them back home ... and fast!

Chapter 5

Several bonfires lit up the beach as Mack and Brady ran down the shoreline. Brady scanned the beach intently.

"If you're looking for this to make sense," Mack began, "you're on the wrong beach."

Brady shook his head. "I'm looking to see if Les Camembert is building his diabolical weather machine."

Mack scrunched up her nose. "How often do you hear that sentence?"

"Remember I told you about a maniacal real-estate developer?" Brady asked.

"Or *that* sentence?" Mack said.

Brady didn't respond. He ran faster as Mack kept up with his frantic pace.

"Les Camembert knows that beachfront property is going to be gold someday," Brady said, panting. "And he begs Big Momma to sell her burger joint so he can build an overpriced resort. But she says no."

Mack threw up her hands. "Of course she does, or there would be no movie."

"He then tries to bribe the bikers and surfers into leaving," Brady continued, "so Big Momma won't have any customers and would have to sell it to him."

"Let me guess," Mack said. "It doesn't work?"

"Of course not," he replied. "They each want Big Momma's for themselves." He stopped running and pointed to a lighthouse up ahead. "I knew it. There! It's the Camembert hideout!" Brady exclaimed. "It's so cool! Let's go!"

Mack and Brady ran past a few more bonfires. One group even had a conga drum, and the beat urged them on as they made their way to the abandoned lighthouse.

"This is it," Brady finally said as they arrived at the lighthouse door.

"But how do we get in?" Mack asked.

Brady smiled and gestured down at his feet. In front of the door was a doormat that read NOT WELCOME. Brady lifted the mat and showed Mack a large skeleton key.

Mack shrugged her shoulders as Brady proudly slipped the key in the lock. The door led to a tunnel that was dark and dank ... and dripping with slime. Mack grimaced as she inhaled an awful smell.

"Seriously?" she asked. "Did somebody burn a gym sock?" She sniffed again. "In cheese?"

"I think I just saw a rat holding his nose," Brady commented.

Mack and Brady reached the end of the tunnel, which opened up into a large laboratory. Les Camembert was standing in front of a machine, looking at its many switches and levers. Another man in a white lab coat was next to him.

"That's him," Brady said, pointing to Les. "He's all British and proper, but he's from Pittsburgh." He watched the two men for a moment. "Desperate to get Big Momma's, Les Camembert hires a mad scientist, Dr Fusion, to carry out his diabolical idea," Brady explained. "Come on," he said, spotting a better area for spying on the men.

The two of them ducked low and scampered across the room without being seen. Mack gawked at the drawings, scientific data and huge old computers scattered around. She stared at the man in the white lab coat with the crazy hair. Dr Fusion was perfectly cast in the role of 'mad scientist'. He was tinkering with the machine while Les talked to him.

"This machine will so drastically change weather patterns," Les boomed, "it will literally still the oceans so there's no longer surf. It'll create humidity so dense, it will rust every piece off all those shiny chrome bikes." He lifted his arms. "The surfers will leave to find a new spot to surf, the bikers won't come near this area ever again and I shall triumph! TRIUMPH, I say!"

Just then, the evil duo broke into a song-and-dance routine. As he sang, Dr Fusion began turning the knobs and flipping all the switches on the machine. It began to make rhythmic noises that got louder and odder as their song went on. By the end, the machine was going crazy, the noise was deafening and smoke was everywhere!

The smoke from the machine made Mack start coughing uncontrollably. Brady grabbed her and pulled her into the tunnel before they were discovered.

"Okay, so in the movie, Lela and Tanner discover Les's plan, unite the bikers and surfers and then destroy the machine, which causes an explosion," Brady said. "That's what creates the storm."

"So, if Lela and Tanner don't get together, which would get the movie back on track the way it's supposed to play out...." Mack said.

"Then the chain of events that create that storm won't happen," Brady finished for her.

"Then we'll be stuck here!" Mack cried. "And never get home!"

"Don't worry," Brady assured her. "We'll figure it out."

"How about figuring it out *while* I worry?" Mack said. Just then, she almost slipped on the slimy floor of the tunnel. Brady caught her just in time. But she wasn't sure he was going to be able to save her from this new movie ending!

Chapter 6

Mack and Brady walked back to the beach area in front of Big Momma's restaurant. The surfers and the bikers had each built their own separate bonfire and were hanging out around them.

Lela came running up to Brady. "Thanks again for catching me, Brady," she said sweetly. Then she looked at both Mack *and* Brady. "Oh, bonkers. Are you two together? I'd never take another girl's boy. That would be stealing," she said. "And probably *really* hard to return."

Mack couldn't help but smile at Lela's words. Then she had a fantastic idea. "No," she said. "I mean, we're together, but we're not *together*."

Brady looked confused. "Lela, this is McKenzie," he said slowly.

"So you won't mind if Brady takes me for a walk on the beach?" Lela asked, her eyes wide.

Mack hesitated, but then thought of her new plan. "Please," she said eagerly. "Beaches were meant to be walked on. Otherwise, they'd be called...." She stumbled over her words as she realized how ridiculous she sounded. "Well, they'd still be called beaches."

Lela looked at Mack. "You guys are strange. I like that. Meet you at the water, Brady," she called as she walked off.

"I don't get it," Brady said, turning to Mack. "First you break up with me, then you push me into the arms of someone else."

"Brady, she's crushing on you," Mack explained.

Brady ran his hands through his hair. "But I like *you*," he said. "And until you've actually gone off to that school, I'm not going to like anyone but you, I mean, the way I like you."

Reaching out to him, Mack looked up into his eyes. "I like you, too," she told him. "But you're not seeing what's right in front of you."

"*You're* right in front of me!" he cried.

Mack pointed towards Tanner, who was walking down the beach, holding a guitar. "Brady, I can explain it to you, but I can't *understand* it for you," she said.

Brady tried to follow where Mack was going with all this. He saw Lela by the water and Tanner on the other side of the beach. Suddenly, he understood. "So the way to get her to like him," he said, pointing to Tanner, "is for me to spend time with *her* so I can deflect her affections off of *me* and on to *him*."

Mack patted him on his shoulder. "I sure hope so. I'll do the same with Tanner."

"Fine," Brady said with a fake sigh. "I'll be back as soon as I can get that smokin' girl to hate me." He shrugged. "The things I do for women."

As Brady went to catch up with Lela, Mack

had a moment of doubt. Should they really do this? But she pushed those thoughts out of her head and headed over to Tanner.

"Hi!" she exclaimed. "Mind if I join you?"

"Of course not," Tanner told her. "I'd want to join me, too." He picked up his guitar and started strumming a few chords.

"So, you play guitar?" Mack asked, trying to strike up a conversation.

"I know," he replied.

This was going to be harder than she thought! She sighed and then tried again. "No, I meant.... You good?" She motioned to Tanner's guitar.

"Sure, when I'm inspired," Tanner said. He lowered his voice and quoted, " 'If music be the food of love, play on.' "

Mack was speechless. She hadn't expected such a deep and thoughtful response! "Was that Shakespeare?" she asked.

"No, that was me," he said. "Sometimes I talk low, for effect."

Mack smiled at him, charmed. "It works."

Tanner shrugged. "I can do high also, but the chicks really dig low better."

Brady and Lela walked along the shore. Brady couldn't have picked a more gorgeous setting for a moonlit stroll.

"So you've never been around here before?" Lela asked.

"No, but have you ever gone someplace that you've never been?" he asked. "But felt like you've been there a million times?"

"I thought I did once," Lela told him. "Then it turned out I was never there."

Brady kicked the sand off the tops of his feet and chuckled. Lela was just like she was in the movie – honest, sweet, and very cute in a vintage bikini.

"But someday I'd love to go someplace I've never been," Lela confessed. "I'm just always ... here."

"It's not a bad place to be," Brady added.

Lela stopped walking and faced Brady. "It's even better now that you're here."

"Wow," Brady said, his hand on his heart. "You really *are* exactly like you!"

Lela laughed and playfully tossed her long hair.

"Lela, how come you bikers don't get along with the surfers?" Brady asked, changing the subject.

"It's always been like that," she explained. "We're not supposed to have a lot in common. Plus, we both want Big Momma's."

"But some of them seemed really cool. Like, oh, that guy Tanner," he said.

Lela didn't take the bait. Instead, she turned her gaze to Brady. "It was very courageous of you to charge the stage and save my life."

"Courageous? Please," he said. "No. *Maybe*. I'm sure anyone would have done the same. Even a surfer."

"You're my hero," she exclaimed.

Brady blushed. "Hero? Well, sure, I guess, but...." He stopped talking, realizing he was getting away from his and Mack's plan. He had to bring the conversation back to Tanner. "Lela, it's amazing to spend time with you, but it's not ... I'm not what you think."

"I dig you, Mack," Tanner declared to Mack as he stared at her. "You're different than the other girls around here."

"No. I'm not different," Mack scoffed. "In fact, I'm totally the same."

"The same as what?" Tanner asked.

"As everyone who *isn't* different," she said, trying to keep to her agenda of getting Tanner to notice Lela.

Her comment went over Tanner's head. "You mind if I write a song for you?" he asked out of the blue.

"Yes! I mean, what rhymes with Mack? Sack?"

she said nervously. "See, bad song. Besides, you think you like me because running into you was destiny. But it is not our destiny. *Your* destiny, with someone you're *meant* to be with, which *isn't* me. See?" She knew that she was talking way too fast for Tanner, but she was desperate to get him to stop liking her.

Tanner just smiled at Mack. He began playing his guitar and singing a song.

Across the beach Lela was singing the same song to Brady. As hard as Mack and Brady tried to convince Tanner and Lela that their soulmates were still out there, it was clear that they didn't believe it! And Brady was finding it difficult not to get totally swept up in the song. He'd had a crush on Lela since the first time he saw her on screen.

When the song ended, Tanner and Lela walked off in opposite directions, leaving Mack and Brady alone. Mack saw Brady on the beach and walked up to him.

"I'm thinking that didn't go as we'd hoped," Brady said.

"And now Tanner really likes me," Mack said. "So what do we do? You're the one who knows this movie so well!"

Brady thought for a moment. "In the movie, the next thing that happens is the biker girls have a pyjama party and the surfer guys all hang at Big Momma's." He paused and then snapped his fingers. "Maybe we need to get ourselves invited."

Mack was happy to have a new plan. She had to find Lela.

Tons of surfers were on the beach in front of Big Momma's restaurant. The wooden porch was packed with kids waiting to eat or just hanging out. Finally, she saw Lela down by the water.

"Hey, Lela," Mack said, running up to her. "You know what I've never done?" She came up next to her and gave her a big smile.

"Eaten a rock? Kissed a squirrel?" Lela asked, giggling.

Mack laughed. "All exciting things," she replied. "But no. I've never had a pyjama party."

"We do them all the time," Lela replied. "We're doing one tonight."

A smile spread across Mack's face. "You don't say?"

"Sure I do. I just did," Lela said.

Just then, Brady spotted Tanner. He knew this was his cue. He walked over to the surfer. "Hey, Tanner," he called. "What are you guys all doing later?"

"Hangin' at Big Momma's. Want to join?" Tanner replied.

Brady was very pleased with himself. "Sure!" he shouted. He walked back over to Mack smugly. "Girls tend to overcomplicate things." He nodded towards Lela with a cocky look in his eyes. "Hey Lela, you should invite Mack to your sleepover."

"Great idea!" Lela cried. "How about it, Mack?"

Mack rolled her eyes at Brady. "I wouldn't

MACK LOVES TO SURF MORE THAN ANYTHING, AND SHE'S AWESOME AT IT!

BRADY IS UPSET WHEN HE FINDS OUT THAT MACK HAS TO LEAVE.

MACK AND BRADY MEET THE BIKER GANG FROM *WET SIDE STORY*.

THE SURFERS AND THE BIKERS ARE SWORN RIVALS.

TANNER IS SUPPOSED TO FALL FOR BIKER CHICK, LELA ...

... BUT HE FALLS FOR MACK INSTEAD!

MEANWHILE, LELA FALLS FOR BLOND-HAIRED BRADY.

LELA TELLS MACK HER BIG SECRET –
SHE WANTS TO TRY SURFING!

THE BIKER GIRLS INVITE MACK
TO THEIR PYJAMA PARTY.

BRADY HANGS OUT WITH TANNER AND THE SURFER GUYS.

MACK AND BRADY CAN'T STOP SINGING AND DANCING!

THEY HAVE TO FIX THE PLOT OF THE MOVIE IF THEY WANT TO GET BACK HOME.

LELA AND TANNER FINALLY REALIZE THEY ARE PERFECT FOR EACH OTHER.

THE SURFERS AND THE BIKERS WORK TOGETHER TO SAVE THEIR BEACH!

WHEN MACK AND BRADY HEAD HOME, EVERYONE IS SAD TO SAY GOODBYE.

miss it," she said. Then something caught her eye that took her breath away. "Be right back." She ran over to her surfboard, which was leaning against the porch railing. She pointed to where her surfing rash guard had been hanging earlier. It was starting to fade away ... fast!

"You *did* see that, right?" Brady asked when the spandex shirt disappeared.

"If you did," Mack said, trying hard to remain calm. "What's going on?"

Brady took a step back. "I don't know," he said slowly. "Maybe because rash guards didn't exist yet, they can't be here, so they disappear."

"But *we* also didn't exist, so...." Mack's voice trailed off. Once again, she couldn't find the right words. She took a deep breath. "What's going to happen to us?" For the first time since they had travelled back in time, Mack's eyes welled up with tears. She wanted to bury herself deep in the sand. Brady reached out to hug her.

In the distance, Mack heard a few chords of music. She pulled back from Brady. "No! No music!" she shouted. "Brady, we have to get out of here," she pleaded. "I have to get on that plane!"

The music started to get louder.

"No! This is not a song!" Mack shouted.

Suddenly, the music stopped.

Mack took a deep breath. She had to get control. She had a sleepover to attend – and a musical to fix!

Chapter 7

In Lela's bedroom, a group of girls lounged around in pyjamas. Struts, one of the biker chicks, was teasing Cheechee's hair up with a comb and hairspray. Mack watched, amazed at what was considered a cool hairstyle in the 1960s.

Lela was standing in front of her wardrobe with her hands on her hips. Rifling through her many hangers, she finally grabbed a dress. She held it up and then slipped it on.

"Should I wear this to see Brady?" she asked. "He loves to surf, and water is blue, and this dress is blue, so next time he surfs, he'll see the blue water and think of me!"

"Why should a boy influence what you decide to wear?" Mack asked. "Or anything you do? It's your life, you should decide what you do," she said. "Besides, boys aren't that smart. That's why they're not girls."

"They only have to be smart enough to ask us out," Cheechee joked.

"Why can't you ask *them* out?" Mack asked.

"We can't ask someone out," Struts said, confused.

Mack stood up and walked over to the girls. "You can do anything a boy can do," she said.

"I don't know where you're from, but around here, you have to ask a boy out *without* asking him," Lela explained. "Like, with your eyes." She demonstrated fluttering her eyelashes.

Mack started to laugh, and Cheechee and Struts joined in. Mack fell back on Lela's bed. This was definitely a very girly slumber party!

Meanwhile, Brady was at Big Momma's with Tanner, Seacat and Rascal. They were playing pool and listening to songs on the jukebox.

"So really, all you guys do around here is eat, hang and surf?" Brady asked.

The surfer boys all nodded their heads. "Yup," they said in unison.

Brady smiled and leaned back in his seat. "Sounds kind of perfect."

"Is there any other way?" Tanner asked.

"There sure are some boo-ha *beauties* around here," Brady said, trying to steer the conversation. "Like that girl who was singing ... Lela?"

"The *Rodent*?" Seacat said. "We don't date no rats."

"You wouldn't take out a girl just because she's a biker?" Brady said.

"The *tide* wouldn't take out a girl just because she's a biker," Seacat said, laughing.

Brady noticed that Tanner seemed a little uncomfortable. "Don't listen to those guys," Tanner said, leaning close to him. "It don't matter if a girl's a surfer, a biker or a bookworm."

"So, what is it you *do* like?" Brady asked the surfers.

"Any girl who agrees to go out with me is the perfect girl!" Rascal exclaimed.

Tanner laughed along with the others but then grew serious. "A chick's got to have something special, you know...."

Brady knew what was most likely coming next – a song. He guessed that Mack was probably being serenaded by Lela and her friends, too.

When Brady and Mack met up the next morning they both did a double take.

"Groovy outfit," Brady joked, pointing to Mack's '60s-style clothes and hairdo.

"You too, Elvis," Mack countered. She had to giggle at Brady's retro hair style. "How'd it go last night?"

Brady grinned. "It was so cool being one of those guys, even for a night," he said. "They look out for each other."

"Well, those girls sure like to talk about boys," Mack said. "But no matter how hard I tried to get Lela to talk about Tanner, I don't think we're any closer than we were before." She took Brady's hand. "What if we can't get them together? We could be stuck here forever."

"Would it be so bad?" Brady said. "For a while, anyway?"

"Yes!" Mack argued. "Every minute that I'm here is another minute I'm not doing what my mum wanted me to do."

Brady put his hand on Mack's shoulder. "But, every minute that we're here, we're still together," he said.

"I know," Mack said with a sigh. "But...."

"Besides, when will we ever get another chance to be in a movie?" he questioned her. "Like, actually *in* a movie. Really, Mack, what's your hurry to grow up – and leave?"

Mack looked down at her toes in the sand. "Everyone's counting on me to."

"But is that really what *you* want?" he asked.

"I thought you understood," she whispered.

"I do," Brady said.

"Then help me get home," Mack said. "Please."

Brady nodded. "Maybe we need to get Lela and Tanner to spend time together without peer pressure."

"Right. So they get to know each other as people, not rivals," she told him.

"How do we do that?" Brady asked.

"I don't know, but I'm not going to stop until I figure it out," Mack said. She spotted Tanner by the water with his surfboard. She jumped up and grabbed her board.

Brady was left in the sand, watching Mack head off to the ocean. He wondered how this was going to end.

When Tanner and Mack finished surfing, they strolled up the beach together. "No one has ever beaten me on the waves," Tanner said to Mack. Tanner was impressed with Mack's surfing skills.

"*Especially* not a girl," he noted, smiling.

"Girls can do anything boys can do," Mack replied. She winked at him. "And we look better doing it."

Tanner threw his head back and laughed. "If I was going to think something right now, I think I'd think that maybe people aren't always what I think."

"Does that go for bikers, too?" Mack asked.

Tanner shifted his surfboard in his hands. "Truth is, bikers aren't that bad. They want the same thing we want."

Mack stopped and looked at Tanner. "Then why the conflict between you?"

Shrugging, Tanner answered honestly. "It's how it's supposed to be, I guess. Like, it's sort of what everyone expects."

Tanner's reply made Mack think. She looked down the long beach. "It's like your heart tells you one thing, but you feel like you have to do something else," she said.

"That's why people who don't follow their hearts, leave their hearts behind," Tanner said.

For the first time since she had met him, Mack saw that he was deeper than just some surfer dude. "You're a pretty smart guy," she said.

"Yeah, but more pretty," Tanner replied, flashing a stellar smile. Then he ran off towards Big Momma's and left Mack standing in the sand.

Tanner's words had made a big impression on Mack. She stood for a moment, letting his advice sink in.

Chapter 8

That evening, Mack was back in Lela's bedroom. She was trying to put a record on the record player. She had no idea how the machine worked!

Lela came up behind her and took the record out of her hands. She placed it on the turntable and lowered the needle. "I know," she said, "this electronic stuff can be really complicated."

Mack laughed to herself. If only Lela knew how she usually played music! When the record started, Mack walked over to the window and gazed at the night sky.

"Are you okay?" Lela asked her.

"Sure ... just homesick," Mack said sadly.

"Is it the decor?" Lela asked, a little horrified.

"No, I'm not sick of *your* home," Mack quickly explained. "I'm...." She didn't want to get into the whole story, so she changed the subject. "So, how are things going with Brady?"

"Good, I guess," Lela said, slightly distracted. "How are things going with Tanner?"

"Good, I guess," Mack replied.

Lela picked up her brush and began combing her hair. "Sometimes I think boys don't tell us what they're thinking, mostly because thinking would involve *more* thinking," she said. "But they make up for it by being cute. And boys."

Mack couldn't help but smile at Lela's simple honesty. She noticed Lela's necklace. It had a round medallion with a rose engraved in the centre. "That's a really pretty necklace."

"It's Hawaiian," Lela told her. "It means 'friendship forever'. Like us, now."

"Lela ... you're not at all what I thought you'd be," Mack told her.

"Yeah, I'm a lot less like me than people think," she said, laughing. "It's funny, I feel like I can tell you anything."

Mack nodded. "I know, it does feel like that."

Suddenly, Lela's eyes grew wide and she let out a yelp. She scurried over closer to Mack. "I have a secret I've never told anyone!"

"I'd be happy to be your 'anyone' if you want," Mack offered.

"Okay. Ready?" Lela asked. She squeezed Mack's hands and then closed her eyes tightly as if she were making a wish on a birthday cake. "I want to surf."

"Surf? Really!" Mack exclaimed.

"I mean, like a pro!" Lela exclaimed. "It's insane, I know. And if my brother found out, he'd blow a gasket." She stood up. "Plus, no girl ever surfed like a boy, until you!" She saw Mack staring at her. "You think I'm crazy, right?"

Mack stood up, too. "Not at all. Lela, never let anyone tell you that you can't do what you want in life."

"But, how do you do that?" Lela asked.

Mack paused for a moment. "It's not always easy," she said. "Believe me!"

"So you think I should surf?" Lela pressed on. "Like you do, like the surfers do?"

A fantastic idea popped into Mack's head. "I think you should definitely surf like the surfers do! In fact, Brady could teach you. He taught me everything I know and I'm a great surfer, right?"

Lela clapped her hands together. "You think he would?"

"I think he'll agree. It's a perfect plan!"

The next morning, Lela was on a surfboard, wading into the shallow water. Brady stood beside her, giving her directions.

"This is so exciting!" Lela gushed. "I'm really going to surf."

"That's the goal," Brady said.

"Mack told me I should believe in myself," she told him. "Thank you for not laughing at me for wanting to do this."

"Hey, you haven't tried yet," Brady said, smiling. "We may *both* be laughing!"

Lela giggled and followed Brady's lead deeper into the water.

In the abandoned lighthouse, Les and Dr Fusion were still working on their weather machine.

"Momentarily, this machine will create enough humidity to cause excessive precipitation, inducing torrential rain, as well as lots of frizzy hair and stinky pits," the mad scientist said. His eyes twinkled with delight. "Now, we just flip this switch...." A light flashed on. "That's better. I could hardly see," he said.

Les rolled his eyes. The suspense was maddening! "Now, we flip *this* switch ever so delicately so as to protect the intricate inner workings...." Dr Fusion mumbled.

He flipped the other switch, but nothing happened. Tilting his head, he thought for a minute, and then he banged the machine hard with his fist. The machine whirled into action!

Mack searched the beach as she walked along the shore. Finally, she spotted Tanner and strolled over to him.

"You know what I would love?" she asked him. "A walk on the beach!" She pointed towards the water where Brady and Lela were having their surfing lesson. "In that direction," she added.

Tanner nodded and then handed her a flower garland for her hair.

Mack was touched. "You made this? For me?" she said, blushing. "Really?"

"There are, like, over a hundred kinds of flowers indigenous to this region, which would look so rad on a foxy babe like you," he said as he put the garland in her hair.

Mack lowered her eyes. "Thanks," she said, gently touching the flowers in her hair. "It's beautiful."

"So, how about that walk?" Tanner asked.

Down at the shore, Brady and Lela ventured farther into the water for their surfing lesson.

"You really think I can do this?" Lela asked.

"Sure," Brady said. "Remember, think of it like riding a bike." Then he thought a moment. "Except without the handlebars. Or bike."

Brady looked up the beach and saw Mack and Tanner coming closer. As they approached, Brady overheard their conversation.

"It's like I say: if you want to meet new people, try taking off on the wrong wave!" Mack exclaimed.

"Exactly!" Tanner replied. "I dig the way you think. And you do it, like, all the time!"

Mack motioned to Brady and he took his cue. He turned to Lela. "Okay, here comes a nice one," he said, pointing at the building wave.

"Just visualize yourself riding it."

Lela was nervous, but she readied herself. "Okay, whatever you say," she said.

"Paddle!" Brady shouted to Lela.

Lela was on her stomach, paddling out to push past the breaking waves. She stood up at the right time and rode the wave in!

"I did it!" she cried as she swam up to Brady.

Mack knew she had to hurry to make her plan work. Tanner still hadn't noticed that Lela was on a surfboard. Mack started to wave and point. "Oh, hey, there's Brady in the water," Mack said. She posed a question as innocently as she could. "And who is that beautiful girl surfing with him?"

Tanner squinted and tried to make out who was surfing. He brought his hand up to his eyes to block the sun's glare. "Wow," he said. "Check that out. She's surfing. Amazing!"

Just as Lela stood up on the board, a beam

from the lighthouse hit the ocean. Dr Fusion's machine began to shoot rays of light out of the lighthouse windows! The machine was beginning to have an effect on the water.

There was a low rumble and suddenly the water went flat and still. Lela looked round, confused. Where were the waves? What happened?

Mack and Tanner both looked out at Lela standing on the motionless surfboard.

Mack caught Brady's eye and they shared a worried look. They both knew that the weather machine was responsible for what had just happened. They had to destroy that machine – and fast!

"Sorry, Lela," Brady said, apologizing. "I guess that's all the surfing for today."

"It's okay. There'll be another time," Lela said optimistically. She looked at the shoreline and spotted Tanner. She recognized him from Big Momma's. She held his gaze for a moment and smiled.

"Bravo!" Les shouted to Dr Fusion as they stood before the weather machine. "So, now that we've temporarily caused these changes in the weather, how do we make them permanent and get rid of the bikers and surfers for good?" he asked.

"We need to magnify the power," Dr Fusion told him. He made his way over to a small cooler and took out a glowing green liquid.

"Plutonium?" Les guessed.

Dr Fusion shook his head. "Lime soda," he said, opening the top and taking a swig from the bottle. Then he reached in and took out another cylinder. This one was filled with red liquid.

"Strawberry soda?" Les asked. Suddenly, he was very thirsty. He grabbed the bottle and took a huge gulp of the drink.

"Plutonium," Dr Fusion said flatly as he took the bottle from Les' hand.

Les spat out the red liquid as Dr Fusion poured the rest of the plutonium into the machine.

"In two hours' time, it will turn green and reach a boiling point of 647 degrees," Dr Fusion explained. "Or, as we scientists like to call it: *Wow that's hot.*"

"Meanwhile, let's go see the effect it had on the water," Les suggested.

They both headed out of the lighthouse, anxious to see if their experiment was working.

"I thought for sure that would work," Mack said, disappointed. She was sitting with Brady on a quiet part of the beach.

"I know," Brady said. "And it was the final warning before the big storm." He looked towards the lighthouse. "Les's plan is working."

Mack looked around and then climbed up a rock to get a better view. "We have to get into that lighthouse again and try to stop them," she said. She thought for a moment. "But we need the element of surprise. You think there's a way in from the water?"

Just then, she slipped and fell off the rock, tumbling right into the ocean! The flower garland fell off her head and landed on the sand. Brady reached his hand out and pulled her up.

"Are you okay?" he asked.

When she stood up, Mack flipped her hair back to get the water out of her face, but she stopped. In a panic, she felt her head. "Hair!" she cried. She pointed to her dry hair. "Hair! Hair!"

Brady stared blankly at her as she ranted on and on about her hair.

"Hair? Hairstyle? Hair extensions?" he asked, trying to figure out what she was getting at. "Hair dryer?"

The word 'dryer' seemed to strike a chord with Mack, so Brady stopped. "Hair dryer *what*?"

Mack didn't answer. Instead, she ran into the water, dunked her hair again and came out.

"Your hair isn't wet," Brady said, realizing what Mack was trying to tell him. "What does it mean?"

"It means my hair isn't wet!" Mack cried. "We're morphing into the movie. We're changing!"

Brady was still confused. "We're changing?"

"We're changing," Mack repeated. "What are we going to do?"

All of sudden, music started playing and Mack began singing. It was as if she couldn't control the words coming out her mouth!

Brady's mouth hung open as he watched and listened to Mack sing about how she felt.

"Why are you singing?" he finally asked.

"I don't know," Mack said. "I suddenly just...."

"... broke into song," he finished for her.

"Oh no! I'm in an involuntary musical number!" she cried.

"Stop," Brady suggested.

"I CAN'T STOP!" Mack shouted between

lyrics. Her emotions were tumbling out in song, and all her thoughts and feelings were creating a moving, heartfelt ballad.

"This isn't good," Brady said, shaking his head. "First the rash guard vanishes, then your hair, now this."

When the song finally ended, Mack cautiously tried to speak.

"Did it stop?" Mack asked. She was so thankful to hear a spoken sentence come out of her mouth and *not* a line from a song.

"I don't know," Brady replied, looking around. "Give it a second."

They both stayed quiet for a long moment, waiting for a musical cue.

"Okay, I think it's passing." Mack listened intently and then sighed with relief. "We're not singing anymore."

"Let's go find Lela and Tanner," Brady suggested. "We have to get them together so they can find out about Les's weather machine and then unify everyone to destroy it before it destroys them!"

"Oh no! We're talking in plot points," Mack said, flinching.

They began to run but stopped short when Les and Dr Fusion appeared in front of them, blocking their way. The doctor aimed a toylike laser gun directly at them.

"Going somewhere?" Les hissed.

"Yes, but it has nothing to do with your diabolical plan to get rid of the surfers and bikers," Mack said. Her hand shot up to her mouth. She didn't mean to tell them that!

"And to destroy Big Momma's forever," Brady added, wincing.

He turned to Mack. "I hate talking in plot points."

"It seems you two miscreants have become a liability to the strategy I've carefully orchestrated," Les said to them.

A few bars of sinister music played off in

the distance, underscoring the dire situation. Mack cringed.

"In just under two hours, this area will all be mine!" Les cackled.

"And how are you going to stop us from warning our friends?" Brady prodded him.

Dr Fusion aimed his laser gun at a rock and fired it. The rock sizzled and disintegrated!

"And now we know," Mack said.

"I should warn you, I know karate," Brady stated. "And, like, two other Japanese words." He leaped towards the gun, but Dr Fusion fired. Brady was thrown back onto the sand.

"Brady! Are you okay?" Mack cried, rushing over to him.

"Oh, he's fine," Dr Fusion said. "It was only a stun gun."

Brady sat up and shook his head. "Wow. In the movie, that looked like it would hurt a whole lot less," he said.

Mack gently helped Brady stand up and

steadied him on his feet. Les and Dr Fusion led them down the beach at gunpoint. Mack glanced over at Brady, who shared the same worried expression. They had no choice but to head to the lighthouse – and see where this new plot point was going to take them!

Chapter 9

Lela ran down the shoreline, weaving in between the sunbathers lying on blankets. She stopped at the ocean's edge and turned round to scan the beach. More than anything, she wanted another surfing lesson today. She had to find Brady! She and was about to give up when she spotted Tanner. He seemed to be searching for someone as well. Lela went up to him, thinking that maybe they could help each other.

"You waiting for Mack?" Lela asked.

"Yeah," Tanner said. "You waiting for Brady?"

"Yeah," Lela said, still looking around. "We're going to surf."

Tanner raised his eyebrows. "What? *You* like to surf?" he asked.

"It's like riding a cloud," Lela said dreamily. She gazed out into the ocean with a faraway expression on her face. Then she chuckled. "Except that cloud is water."

"No way," Tanner said, pointing his thumb at his chest. "I said that same thing, except not right now."

"I know bikers aren't supposed to like surfing, but I don't care," Lela cried.

"You don't?" Tanner asked. He moved closer to her. The biker chick he had seen hanging around Big Momma's suddenly looked different to him. "Hey. You know what? I've always wanted to ride a motorcycle," he confessed.

"Are you *serious*?" Lela asked. She eyed the surfer boy curiously.

"No. I'm Tanner," he said with an absolutely straight face.

"I grew up riding," Lela told him.

"Is that why you're stunning as a moon that lighteth up a day?" Tanner asked, using his low, poetic voice.

"Who said that?" Lela asked, impressed.

"I just did," Tanner said. He stood up tall and proudly.

"Wow. I really like your low voice."

"Thanks. I can do high, too."

Lela smiled. "Who'd have thought a biker and a surfer could have so much in common?" She looked down at the sand and then up at Tanner again. "Did you ever think the person you thought was perfect for you isn't as perfect as the *perfect* person for you?"

"You mean ... you?" Tanner said sweetly.

"And you," she added coyly.

Tanner and Lela started to sing about destiny and belonging together. Suddenly, the whole beach was involved in a full-on dance number! Lela leaped up onto one of the high rocks near the water's edge.

As Lela sang, she suddenly slipped and lost her balance. She wobbled and fell right into Tanner's arms. They looked into each other's eyes ... and kissed.

"Hey, what are we going to tell Mack and Brady?" Lela asked, still feeling the electricity of their kiss.

"Yeah, where are they anyway?" Tanner said, looking around. Suddenly, Tanner saw the flower garland he gave to Mack lying on the sand. He picked it up and showed it to Lela.

"I gave this to Mack. She was wearing it," he said, thinking out loud.

"Why would she take it off?" Lela wondered.

"Something's not right!" Tanner cried.

They looked at each other and then towards the abandoned lighthouse. Suddenly, everything clicked into place. They remembered the crazy property developer who had once tried to bribe the surfers and bikers to leave Big Momma's. Then they thought about the ray from the lighthouse that had stopped the waves. Tanner and Lela realized it all must be connected!

"We need to get help," Lela declared.

"But from who?" Tanner asked.

The new couple raced up the beach to find help. They needed to figure out how to save Mack and Brady – and fast!

Mack and Brady were tied up in the villains' laboratory. They watched as Dr Fusion worked on the weather machine, making small adjustments to knobs and levers.

"In mere moments, less time than it takes for me to steal this scene," Les announced, "this machine will change the weather patterns. I will take possession of Big Momma's and all your friends will disappear forever – or longer!" Les laughed maniacally.

"There's one flaw with your plan!" Mack called over to him.

"And what might that be?" Les asked, turning to look at his prisoners.

Mack glanced at Brady. She shrugged. "I don't know, isn't there always one flaw with these kind of plans?" she asked.

Les waved her off. "Now I'm off to measure the beach for a resort parking lot," he said as he headed out of the door.

Dr Fusion gave Mack and Brady an evil stare and followed Les outside.

"I guess it could be worse," Brady mused once he was alone with Mack. "At least my favourite movie wasn't *Tarantulas on a Train*."

Mack looked at him, then started to laugh uncontrollably.

"Okay, you've lost it," Brady said.

Mack took a deep breath and grew serious. "Brady, I've spent this entire movie telling Lela to follow her heart and do what she loves," she confessed. "And she did." Mack thought of Lela, a hard-core biker, out on a surfboard having fun. "She has more courage than I do."

"That's not true," Brady told her. He strained to turn and see Mack's face. "You're braver than anyone I know."

"If we hadn't come here," Mack began, "I'd be on a plane right now, heading for some private school to become something I don't really want to be." She felt relieved to finally get that confession off her chest. Then she sighed. "Instead, we're being held prisoner in a lighthouse where a sinister weather machine could destroy a surfer's paradise!"

"So, you're glad we came?" Brady asked.

"I couldn't be more glad!" Mack exclaimed. She grinned at Brady. "It's like, I'm tied up, but at the same time, I've never felt more free." She tilted her head towards Brady. "You were right. What's my hurry to grow up when I could be stuck in 1962 with you?"

Brady struggled to slip his hand into Mack's and give her a reassuring squeeze. Mack rested her head on his shoulder. This might not have been the plot twist she expected, but Mack still wanted to enjoy the moment.

Tanner and Lela burst into Big Momma's. The place was filled with the surfers and bikers having burgers and shakes. As usual, there was tension between the two groups on different sides of the restaurant. Lela and Tanner leaped onto the stage and tried to get everyone's attention.

"Everyone, listen!" Tanner shouted.

All heads in the restaurant turned towards the stage. There was complete silence as the crowd watched the mismatched couple – a surfer boy and a biker chick.

"Les Camembert wants to destroy us!" Lela told the crowd.

"He's built a weather machine that will stop the tide...." Tanner explained.

"... and rust all of our bikes!" Lela finished his sentence. She tried to enlist some support from the crowd. There was a roar from the biker side of the room.

"Just to get rid of us," Tanner added.

Lela looked around at the people in the restaurant. "Plus, he's got Mack and Brady held captive in a secret location." She stepped closer to the edge of the stage. "We need your help."

"Us or them?" Butchy asked, pointing to himself and then to the surfers across the room.

"Us," a surfer cried, standing up.

"I think she meant *us*," one of the bikers replied.

Seacat stood up and looked right at Tanner. "You meant them?"

"Or did you mean *them*?" Cheechee said to Lela, standing up with her hands on her hips.

"I mean *all* of us!" Lela shouted.

"Ohhhhhhhhhh," the crowd replied in a collective sigh.

"The only hope is to work together," Tanner urged everyone. "Free our friends and destroy that machine before it destroys our world."

"Why should we do anything with them?" Butchy asked, eyeing the surfers across the room.

"Hey," Seacat replied, staring down Butchy. "We didn't want to do anything with you first."

"Together we can help each other," Tanner said, focusing the crowd. He was trying to gain support, but no one seemed care.

Butchy walked over to the stage and pointed at Tanner. "Why should we listen to you?" he growled.

Tanner flashed the biker a stellar, sparkling smile. "I never thought I'd have anything in common with a biker either, until I took a ride with one!" He gestured to Lela and held her gaze.

"In fact, all our fighting ever did was stop us from seeing what we have in common," Lela added as she winked at Tanner.

"Big Momma's, the beach and ... us!" Tanner cheered. Lela clasped Tanner's hand and raised it up for the crowd to see. They stood united in front of everyone. The crowd cheered when they realized that the two were now a couple.

Butchy stepped near the stage. No one in Big Momma's breathed a word. Was he going to punch Tanner for touching his sister? Silently, everyone moved in closer to see what would happen next.

After a long moment of silence, Butchy approached Tanner and shook his hand.

Tanner grinned. "Let's go!" Butchy and Tanner shouted in unison. They led the crowd out of the restaurant.

"No running!" Big Momma cried as she saw everyone racing for the door. Then she thought better of it, sensing the urgency of the situation. "Ah, go ahead."

All the surfers and bikers rushed down the beach towards the lighthouse. They were on a mission. And now they were all united!

Chapter 10

Les stood outside of the old lighthouse. He spotted a group of kids running down the beach and grimaced. This was not part of his plan.

Inside the laboratory, Dr Fusion was still holding Mack and Brady at gunpoint.

"Do you really want to do this?" Brady asked the scientist. "Ruin the lives of all these people?"

"Just because you can magnify the power of nuclear plutonium to 647 degrees, doesn't mean you have to," Mack said. Then she noticed Brady staring at her. "What?" she said, shrugging. "It's not like I *never* paid attention when you watched the movie."

Brady couldn't help but laugh.

"How did you know that?" Dr Fusion barked. He moved the toy gun closer to them. "Who are you?" he said, glaring at them.

"Fine," Brady said. If this guy wanted the truth, he would give it to him. "We're from the future and you're not real. You're a villain in a movie we got stuck in somehow."

"No," Dr Fusion said, shaking his head.

"Yup," Mack said.

"Noooooooooooo!" Dr Fusion cried. "So I'm nothing but a flicker on a silver screen, destined to relive the same evil deeds and trite dialogue, over and over?"

"Yeah, pretty much," Mack told him.

Just then, Les ran in from his outside post. "Bad news," he gasped. "The bikers and surfers have united together in order to save you and destroy us."

"How is that bad news?" Brady asked.

Les smirked. "Correction. Bad news for *you*."

He turned to Dr Fusion. "It's time!"

Dr Fusion faced the machine. He hit the glowing red button. Pulsing red rays shot out of the lighthouse, penetrating the sky.

On the beach, Tanner, Lela and Butchy looked up at the laser show. Tanner turned to Butchy.

"Look. Ray!" Tanner called.

"No. *Butchy*," he said, pointing to himself. "Ray is my cousin."

Lela motioned to the cliff where the lighthouse was perched. "No, the ray," she clarified. "It's coming from that lighthouse."

"That must be where they are!" Tanner exclaimed.

Butchy looked up at the creepy lighthouse. "I got to be honest. I'm not big on lighthouses. It's a thing. For some people, it's caves. For some, it's snakes. Me, it's lighthouses!"

All of the surfers and bikers gathered behind Butchy and stared up at the cliff.

Seacat moved through the crowd to stand next

to Butchy. "You can do this. We're all with you," he said. "What do you say?"

Butchy looked round. "Wow," he replied. The group was being so supportive and kind. "My fear is gone!" he exclaimed. "Let's go!"

The gang trekked up the cliff and arrived at the lighthouse. Everyone headed through the dark tunnel into the hidden laboratory. Their entrance took Les and Dr Fusion by surprise.

"Lela!" Brady cried when she burst into the room.

"Tanner!" Mack exclaimed.

"Problem!" Les shouted over the noise.

"We're here to save you," Lela said. Mack and Brady suddenly noticed that Lela and Tanner were holding hands.

"Look at that, Brady," Mack said. "They got together all by themselves."

Brady grinned. "I guess they had to. It was written that way."

The crowd piled in and quickly untied Mack and

Brady. Then, they tied Les and Dr Fusion together!

"You'll never stop us!" Les cried, still trying to fight the crowd. "We will destroy you."

"Annihilate you," Dr Fusion added.

"Discombobulate you!" Les shouted.

Mack picked up the toy ray gun that Les must have dropped in the scuffle. She carefully pointed it at Les and Dr Fusion.

Les quickly changed his tune. "Actually, we're good," he said, backing away.

"Never better," Dr Fusion agreed, looking for a way out of the lab.

"Good luck to you," Les said with a goofy grin.

Just then, the weather machine started shooting rays again and making threatening sounds.

Brady turned to Lela and Tanner. "You have to destroy the machine."

"It's too late!" Les told them. "Say goodbye to this beach as you know it!"

The machine continued to fire pulsing rays. Butchy, Tanner and the other bikers and surfers tried to stop it, but they couldn't figure out which of the many switches to flip.

Lela stepped closer to the machine and quickly assessed the mechanical parts. "Wait!" she cried. "That motor is not much different than the four-stroke, 500-cc, flat-twin, air-cooled Wankel with shaft final and rear-wheel drive." She looked round at the bikers. "That's the kind of motor that you guys refurbish all the time."

Butchy pushed to the front of the crowd. "Let me see," he said. He looked for a second, then reacted. "She's right," he said. "But it's too far down to get to without taking it apart." He held up his pudgy hand. "Especially with these sausage fingers."

Lela smiled. She held up her own slender hand and wiggled her fingers. "Not for me it isn't!" She took a hairpin from her head and approached the machine. Then she reached in and short-circuited the motor in one motion.

Suddenly, there was a low rumble. Smoke escaped with incredible force from a few areas of the machine. The lights flickered and flashed. Everyone backed away as the inevitable eruption built up and up.

"Let's get out of here!" Butchy yelled.

Everyone ran for the exit. As the last of the surfers and bikers left, Dr Fusion and Les realized that they had been left alone in the lab. There was an awkward moment of silence, except for the noise of the weather machine building towards an explosion.

"I can't even imagine a scenario where this turns out well for us," Les said to the scientist.

"Nope," Dr Fusion agreed.

There was a loud pop, and Les and Dr Fusion panicked as the weather machine exploded. The two men went flying out of the lighthouse window, still tied up. They landed out in the ocean, bobbing in the water on a shattered piece of the weather machine.

"I'm not sure I like the way this movie ends," Dr Fusion muttered.

Les looked at him, confused. He scratched his head. "Movie? What movie?"

"Glad you asked," Dr Fusion replied. "It seems we're all in this movie, and we're villains!"

"Intriguing," Les said. "Tell me more...."

Dr Fusion grabbed the weather machine's main lever and used it as a paddle. "Apparently, as we've been carrying out our plot, cameras have been watching," Dr Fusion explained. He glanced over his shoulder. "Of course, had I known, I'd have done something more flowy with my hair." He shook his tangled mess of hair and straightened up a bit. His voice trailed off as he and Les floated farther out into the ocean.

Chapter 11

Mack and Brady found themselves in front of Big Momma's restaurant, confused and slightly winded.

"How did we get back here?" Mack asked. She was just at the lighthouse – and then there was the explosion.

"Because it's exactly where we're supposed to be," Brady replied. "We can leave exactly as we came."

Mack nodded her head. She was starting to understand. All plot points were checked. She and Brady just needed the right wave to ride back to the future and end this story.

"Looks like the movie is back on track," Mack said. "We can leave."

They spotted Lela and Tanner approaching them from further down the beach. The two, clearly in love, were holding hands and smiling at each other. Other surfers and bikers gathered round them as the crowd moved towards Mack and Brady.

Tanner was beaming at Lela. "You did it!" he cheered. He was still blown away by her quick thinking at the lighthouse.

"Of course," Lela said proudly. "Girls can do anything boys can do!"

"Even ... surf," Tanner added, giving Lela a wink.

Brady stepped forwards, moving closer to Lela. "We have to go home," Brady told her.

"Stay," Lela pleaded with him. "You'll love it here. It's always just like this." She motioned to the beach, the waves and all of her friends gathered together. "Perfect."

Tanner faced Mack. "Perfect," he echoed.

Mack nodded her head. "Where I'm going back to is perfect also," she said. She took Brady's hand and gave it a tight squeeze. "I'm going to make sure of it."

Butchy broke through the crowd. "You saved Big Momma's and for that we are, to you, gratefully grateful," he said.

Tanner walked over to Brady. "You rock, bro." He held up his hand for a high five.

Brady saw Mack's face. He shrugged, feeling guilty. "Fine. I *might* have taught him that," he confessed.

"Ever since you both got here, it's been like a different world," Lela said to Mack.

"But not just because of us," Mack replied.

Lela took off her necklace. She reached over to Mack and put it round her new friend's neck.

Mack grabbed the medallion with her fingers, getting a little choked up. "Friendship forever," she said softly.

"Forever," Lela agreed. She pulled Mack in for a tight hug.

Tanner ran and fetched Mack's surfboard. "Kowabunga!" he cried. Mack tucked the board under her arm and faced the water.

"You sure you're ready?" Brady whispered in Mack's ear.

"Yeah," she said, "now that I know what I'm going home to do." She took his hand.

Everyone on the beach watched as Mack and Brady walked towards the water. Mack turned back and took in the view. On the beach, bikers and surfers stood together in harmony. She scanned their faces one more time, letting the moment soak in. She was going to miss everyone, but she had never been more ready to go home.

"Surf's up!" Rascal cried.

All the kids on the beach cheered and waved as Mack and Brady turned to face the incoming waves. The ocean was rumbling with the sound of crashing water. There was a storm coming.

"Okay, are you ready?" Brady asked.

"Let's do it," Mack said, full of confidence.

They started paddling harder. They had to reach the next big wave before it broke in order to travel back to the present day. A huge wave rose up and the two were there to meet it just in time. As they surfed through the barrel, the wave crashed down on them, pulling the pair deep beneath the swirling water.

Chapter 12

The forceful whitecaps pushed in towards the beach. There was no sign of Mack or Brady. Suddenly, Mack's surfboard broke the surface of the water. Seconds ticked by, and then Mack and Brady popped up from under the surf.

"You okay?" Brady asked trying to catch his breath.

Mack lifted her hand up and felt her head. "It's wet! My hair is wet!" she cried. She shook her head happily, feeling the water drip everywhere.

"It is! It's a mop!" Brady replied, laughing. He reached out and touched her head. "A wet, beautiful, stringy mop."

Mack's grandfather was standing on the beach, looking out into the breaking waves. When he saw Mack and Brady bobbing in the water, he cheered. "She's good!" he cried. His shoulders relaxed, and he sighed with relief. "She made it," he whispered to himself with a smile on his face.

The whole crowd on the beach cheered when they saw their friends. Mack and Brady waved happily in reply.

Brady spun his head round. "Hey," he said to Mack. "No time has passed. This is exactly when we left!"

"We did it!" Mack cheered.

"And you still have a chance to ride one of the biggest waves to ever hit this beach," Brady said, looking out to the horizon. The moment that Mack had been waiting for had not passed. "And I promise I won't try and save you."

Mack laughed. "If I needed saving, I'd want you to be the one to do it," she said.

Brady swam over to his Jet Ski. He looked back at Mack and nodded. She had to take this ride by herself.

Swinging her legs over the board, Mack got on and paddled into position. She glanced over her shoulder at Brady. They exchanged a final, knowing look. This was her moment, and Brady knew that Mack was ready.

Mack faced the incoming wave and readied herself on her board. The rose emblem on the front of her board caught her eye. She touched the flower and took a deep breath.

From the shore, she heard a lifeguard's whistle. The lifeguard lowered the red flag and raised a white one, indicating that it was safe to surf again. The crowd on the beach cheered as Mack headed out to conquer the fierce wave.

The wave started to swell. Mack leaped up on her board, expertly slicing into the huge wave. She was spectacular!

Brady proudly watched Mack handle herself

like a pro on the monster wave. She really was an awesome surfer!

The wave began to curl high above her and she skimmed her hand against the inside wall of the perfect barrel. Mack grinned. This was what she loved most about surfing. She was fully in control and loving it!

The crowd on the beach erupted in a chorus of cheers. Mack's ride was incredible.

But as the barrel of the wave closed around her, she disappeared from view. The crowd grew anxious as they waited for Mack to surface. Suddenly, she exploded out of the barrel. It was the perfect finish to a perfect ride!

Mack emerged triumphantly from the water. All the surfers and spectators on the beach ran to greet her as she approached the sand.

Brady raced over, with Mack's grandfather close behind him.

"I'm proud of you McKenzie," her grandfather told her, giving her a huge hug.

"Thanks, Grandpa," she said, looking into his eyes, "for the ride of my life."

At that moment, Aunt Antoinette came storming over to them. She was huffing and puffing, struggling to walk through the sand in high heels. "McKenzie, do you know what you've done?" she shouted.

A smile spread across Mack's face. "Yeah," she said. "I killed on that wave."

"We're late for our flight, late for registration and *totally* off schedule," she snapped. "And all so you could slice a container?"

Brady smirked. "I think you mean 'carve a barrel'," he said, correcting her.

"Thanks, I've got this one," Mack said to Brady. She faced her aunt and took a deep breath. "I love you, Aunt Antoinette," she said. "And Mum would be happy you care so much, but I think you've been wrong. Mum would want me to be happy being successful at what I loved, like you are at what you love." She paused and gestured to her aunt's business attire. "It's just not what *I* love."

Antoinette looked confused. "I'm trying to read between the lines," she said, exasperated.

"I want to finish high school here," Mack told her. "I want to be with Brady, surf more and enjoy myself. Then, well, I don't know what then," she said, laughing. "The thing is, I don't have to know. Not just yet. But whatever it is, it'll be my choice."

"Fine," Antoinette said with a sigh. "Have it your way. You're headstrong, just like your grandfather."

Mack reached out and gave her aunt a hug. "That's the nicest thing you ever could have said," she told her, winking at her grandpa.

Antoinette's face softened a little as she hugged her niece. In her own way, she was giving Mack her approval.

Mack's grandfather smiled. He was proud of his granddaughter – and his daughter.

"Hey, you know what we should do?" Brady asked.

Mack and Brady exchanged a look. They spoke at the same time, but each said something different!

"Surf!" Mack cheered.

"Sing!" Brady exclaimed.

Once again, Mack and Brady found themselves surrounded by a crowd of people singing and dancing. As Mack danced, the necklace that Lela had given her started to glow. In the centre circle of the necklace was a rose emblem, the same as the one on her grandfather's surfboard.

At the end of the song, Mack's grandfather spotted an ice cream cart. "Three chocolate. One sea grass and buckwheat," he told the vendor.

"Just like when we were kids," Antoinette said, grimacing at her father's ice cream choice. "I guess it's nice that some things don't change."

"Hey, Gramps," the ice cream vendor said, "my dad wanted me to tell you, that board you made him helped win him a championship."

"Is that right?" The older man grinned.

"Yup," the ice cream vendor said, handing out the cones. "Heck, half the surfers on this beach wouldn't be who they are if it wasn't for you."

Mack and Brady noticed the old TV on the ice cream cart was playing *Wet Side Story*. The surfers and bikers were gathered on the porch of Big Momma's. Instead of being separated into their usual groups, the crowd was all mixed together. They were smiling and waving as the end of the movie neared. In the final moments, Lela and Tanner kissed and smiled right into the camera. Across the screen, the words 'The End' appeared. Mack and Brady gave each other a knowing smile.

"See!" Mack cried. "Who doesn't love a movie with a happy ending?"

She turned to look at her grandfather, Aunt Antoinette and Brady, who were each enjoying an ice cream cone at the beach. There was no other place in the world she'd rather be!

LOOK OUT FOR THESE AWESOME
TEEN BEACH MOVIE BOOKS!

Activity Book

ISBN 978-1-4723-1931-9

Poster Book
ISBN 978-1-4723-1887-9

Book of Secrets

ISBN 978-1-4723-1932-6